Published by Boyds Mills Press, Inc.

A Highlights Company

815 Church Street

Honesdale, Pennsylvania 18431

Visit our Web site at www.boydsmillspress.com

First published in Great Britain in 2004 by Andersen Press, London.

Color separated in Italy by Fotoriproduzioni Grafiche, Verona.

Printed and bound in Italy by Grafiche AZ, Verona.

Publisher Cataloging-in-Publication Data (U.S.)

Oram, Hiawyn.

Rubbaduck and Ruby Roo / story by Hiawyn Oram ; with pictures by David Lucas. —1st U.S. ed.

[28] p. : col. ill. ; cm.

First published in London : Andersen Press, 2004

ISBN 1-59078-356-5

Summary: When Ruby Roo goes to market to buy seeds for Rubbaduck's garden, she is tricked

by Mischievous Monkey into buying things other than seeds.

1. Toys – Fiction — Juvenile literature. I. Lucas, David, ill. II. Title.

[E] 22   PZ7.O736Ru 2005

First U.S. edition, 2005

This book has been printed on acid-free paper

10   9   8   7   6   5   4   3   2   1

Rubbaduck and Ruby Roo

story by Hiawyn Oram

with pictures by David Lucas

Boyds Mills Press

Rubbaduck was an old rubber duck. He lived with all the world's other old and lost toys.

He had a comfortable little house he'd built himself and a vegetable patch he was very proud of.

Then, one day, there was a knock
at his door. It was Ruby Roo,
the rosy-cheeked rag doll.
   "My child grew up," she said.
"Now what shall I do?"

"You can stay with me for a bit, until you get used to it,"
said Rubbaduck.

So Ruby Roo moved in with Rubbaduck and as soon
as she was settled she began to eat.

She ate everything in the cupboards.
She picked all the vegetables and ate the lot,
boiled or baked, she didn't care.

"Now what shall we have?" she said.
Rubbaduck gasped, rubbed his eyes
and looked in his money tin.

But the tin was empty.

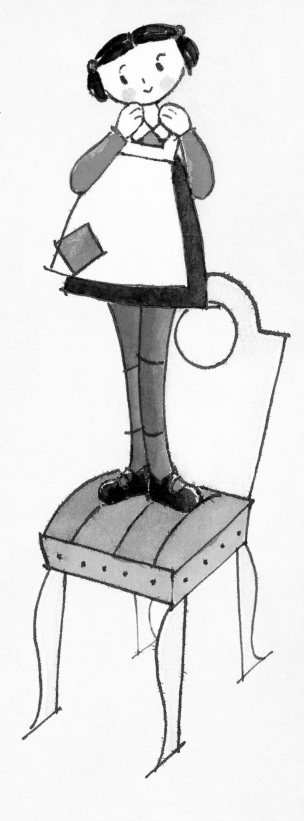

"All right," he sighed, taking out his best coat. "Take this coat to market. Sell it for all the gold you can get so we can buy seeds to plant more vegetables."

So Ruby Roo put the coat over her arm and set off.
But almost at once she met Mischievous Monkey.

"That's a fine coat," he said. "Give it to me and I'll give you
this Magic Dancing Stick. All you have to say is
Dance, Stick, Dance – and it will."

"A Magic Dancing Stick!" cried Ruby Roo.
"Rubbaduck will love that!"
And she exchanged the coat for the Dancing Stick
and went home.

"But we can't plant a Dancing Stick!"
cried Rubbaduck.
    "Then what shall we do?" wailed Ruby Roo.

"Here," sighed Rubbaduck, taking his best hat from the cupboard. "Take this to market. Sell it for all the gold you can get so we can buy more seeds and grow more vegetables."

So Ruby Roo put the hat under her arm and set off.

But almost at once Mischievous Monkey
appeared again.

"That's a fine hat," he said. "Give it to me and I'll give you
this Magic Singing Bee. All you have to do is say
Sing, Bee, Sing – and it will."

"A Magic Singing Bee!" said Ruby Roo.
"Why Rubbaduck will be *oh so* pleased!"
And she exchanged the hat for the Singing Bee
and went home.

But when she got home,
Rubbaduck was NOT pleased.
"No! No! No!" he cried.
"We can't grow a Singing Bee!"
"Then what shall we do?" said Ruby Roo.

"Here," said Rubbaduck, taking his best slippers from the cupboard.
"Take these to market, sell them for all the gold you can get
and don't talk to Mischievous Monkey on the way, whatever you do."

So Ruby Roo put the slippers under her arm and set off.

But almost at once Mischievous Monkey appeared AGAIN.
"Those are fine slippers," he said, "especially the gold tassles.
Give them to me and I'll give you this Magic Fiddle.
All you have to say is *Play, Fiddle, Play* – and it will play all by itself."

"A Magic Fiddle!" cried Ruby Roo. "Why, even Rubbaduck
couldn't say *no* to a Magic Fiddle!" And she exchanged
the slippers and ran all the way home.

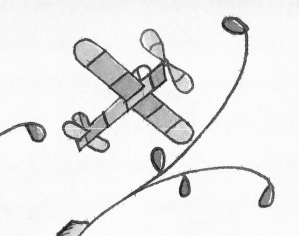

But before Rubbaduck could say one word about
the Magic Fiddle there was a knock at the door.
It was King Lion.

"The Queen hasn't smiled for years," he said.
"And I'm *so* tired of her unsmiling face,
I'm offering this giant bag of gold to anyone
who can make her laugh."

"Ruby Roo," said Rubbaduck,
"I think I have an idea."

Then he took up the Dancing Stick, the Singing Bee and the Magic Fiddle and went over to King Lion's house with Ruby Roo following right behind.

"Dance, Stick, dance!" said Rubbaduck.
"Sing, Bee, sing!" cried Ruby Roo, getting the idea.
And "Play, Fiddle, play!" they both cried together.

And at once – just as Mischievous Monkey said they would –
the Stick danced, the Bee sang, the Fiddle played,
and the Queen Lion laughed till the tears rolled
down her cheeks.

King Lion gave Rubbaduck the giant bag of gold.

Rubbaduck went to market
and bought enough seeds and plants
to turn his whole garden into one enormous
fruit and vegetable patch.

"Oh my!" cried Ruby Roo.
"Peaches and plums and red cherries too!
I knew things would work out between us,
if you gave me a chance!"

"Hmmph," said Rubbaduck smiling shyly. "Maybe . . ."
But Ruby Roo was right.
They did!